MAX&Annie

this Book belongs to:

_____

_____

_____

A company where children have a voice.

www.voiceofkids.com

Text copyright © 1999 by Sandra Philipson
Illustration copyright © 1999 Robert Takatch

Chagrin River Publishing Company
P.O. Box 173
Chagrin Falls, Ohio 44022

First Edition
Printed in the United States of America
10 9 8 7 6 5 4 3 2 1

Library of Congress Catalog Card Number 99 075232
Philipson, Sandra.
Annie Loses Her Leg But Finds Her Way / by Sandra Philipson; illustrated by Robert Takatch
Summary: A Springer Spaniel loses her leg to cancer, but with the help of family and friends she finds that life can still be sweet.
ISBN 1-929821-00-X (hardcover)
[1. Children with cancer–Juvenile Fiction. 2. Children with disabilities–Juvenile Fiction.
3. English Springer Spaniels–Juvenile Fiction. 4. Friendship–Juvenile Fiction. 5. Inspirational story for children–Juvenile Fiction.]

Annie Loses Her Leg but Finds Her Way

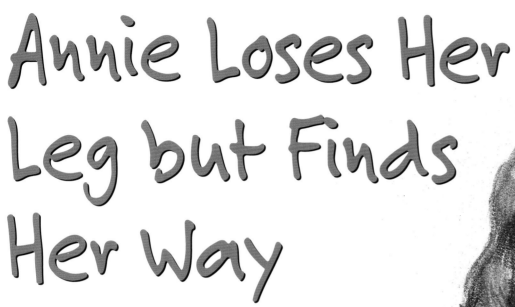

This book is dedicated to the animals who give us their love and friendship and bring fun, wonder, and joy into our lives.

Max, the ever-energetic brown and white Springer Spaniel, barreled through his dog door and slid into the kitchen on his haunches. He skidded to a stop at his mom's feet and looked up at her with his big brown eyes and freckled face, expecting a laugh for his dramatic and noisy entrance. Instead of getting his usual pats and scratches, Max felt Mom grab at his collar. Something was very different in the house tonight. Something was wrong. He could feel it. He thought for a moment and sniffed the air. Annie, his sister Springer, was home from the hospital.

Annie had been gone for two days getting her limp fixed. She had been limping for months and hadn't been able to play or take long walks the way they used to.

"She must be fixed up by now," Max thought. He looked through the kitchen door into the family room, and there she was on her dog bed by the fireplace. From a distance Annie looked all right. Max tugged at his collar, but Mom still held him tight.

"Calm down, Max. Annie just got home from the hospital,"

Mom said as she slowly let go of his collar. Max peeked around the corner.

Then he walked into the family room and over to Annie. She looked up at him with big, sad, sleepy, brown eyes; she didn't get up to greet him.

Immediately Max thought he saw the problem.

Annie had clothes on!

She was dressed in a yellow and black checked flannel shirt, and there was a green fleece coat on the floor beside her.

"Oh, no!" shouted Max.

"Mom is going to start dressing us like that nerdy poodle, Bunny, who lives two houses away. That poodle looks so weird, all clipped, dipped, perfumed, manicured and stuffed into a pink fleece coat. She even has matching booties on her paws for when it is snowy. Everyone thinks it's "precious," but really, it's embarrassing.

We are animals, for gosh sakes—we have perfectly good fur coats, and besides, how can you roll in horse poop and scratch your back on briar bushes if you are packed into a coat like a stuffed sausage?"

"Well, she is not dressing me!" Max went on in a huff. "My brown and white spotted coat is what I wear. I can't believe you are putting up with this, Annie! Not me, no sir. I'm not going to prance around like some fancy, schmancy, over-groomed, poofed up, fluff ball, air-headed poodle. This is awful!" said Max who often talked too much before he really understood a situation. Max had a good heart but also a big mouth that sometimes got him into trouble.

"No wonder you are feeling bad, Annie. And, I hate to say it , but yellow and black aren't your colors. They are not good with your eyes . . . "

"Be Quiet, Max." Annie said with an exasperated sigh.

"I'm wearing the shirt to protect my stitches."

As usual, Max had assumed he knew what was going on without really knowing, and his mouth had gone off talking and talking.

Now he was just getting ready to say something else, when he looked down at Annie. She looked a little different, so he took a quick inventory. He checked out her head—two ears, two eyes, one nose, one mouth, and lots of freckles. Her collar with her I.D. tag was still on; her fur, what he could see of it below the shirt, looked fine. Her cute cropped tail was there. Then he looked at her paws and started counting,

one, two, three, three . . .

Max looked at her frantically and sniffed, "Where is your fourth paw?! Oh, no, where is your whole left leg?" he cried, as he collapsed in a heap in front of her.

"It's gone," she said simply.

"What do you mean gone?" Max demanded. "You went to the hospital to have it fixed, fixed, not taken off! I know it had been hurting you, but you still played anyway. You still jumped on me every night at playtime; you seemed OK," Max went on even more frantically. "Mom thought it was arthritis; Dad said it was bursitis; I thought it was kneeitis—I don't know . . . This is too drastic!"

"It was cancer," Annie said.

"Did you get a second opinion?" Max persisted. "What about medicines, radiation, gene therapy, apricot pits, green tea, acupuncture, alternative medicine? What about tree bark, meditation, mediation, mushrooms, melons, mustard sauce? Couldn't anything save your leg?"

"No, Max. The doctor took off my leg to save my life. Sometimes it is as simple as that, but that doesn't make it easy. Still, I should be able to live a good life, even without my leg. Everyone at the hospital told me that," said Annie a little doubtfully.

Max went off to his dog crate to think things over, and Annie had a treat and drifted off to sleep in front of the fire. She was still tired from the operation.

For the next week, **Max tried his best not to be too obnoxious** while Annie was recovering. Actually he was worried because Annie seemed so sad.

She didn't want to eat her dog food, so every day Mom and Dad took them both
to the fast food place for what they all called

"Annie burger meals."

This was a plain burger, a couple of fries, and a part of a low fat vanilla shake.
This was a nice break from the usual lamb and rice dog food, and certainly
Max enjoyed eating out, but it wasn't any fun if Annie wasn't happy.

Annie got lots of special attention while she was getting better. She got to sleep with Mom and Dad; she got lots of extra petting; she got to sit with Dad in his chair when he watched Monday Night Football; and she got to sit in the front seat of the Jeep almost every time they went for a ride while Max had to stay in back.

Still, Annie was sad.

Then one morning Mom said it was time
to go back to **the river and woods** for their walks.

Annie got in the car slowly and reluctantly; Max bounded into the backseat, as energetic as usual. When they got to the parking lot, another car was there waiting for them. As they got out, a big, beautiful, tall Golden Retriever came bounding up to meet them. The moms were friends; this had all been arranged. The Golden's name was Samantha, and she had three legs too!

"Wow!" barked Max. "She's gorgeous. Look at that coat, that face, those eyes . . ."

"Down boy," said Annie. "Since you turned two, all you think about is girls, Max. Geesh! You stay with Mom, I have some questions I want to ask her."

"Ask her if she thinks I'm cute," whined Max.

Annie and Sam sniffed each other, as dogs do when they first meet. Annie could hardly wait to ask Sam about losing her leg, but before she could, Sam blurted out, "Heard you had cancer. . . so did I. I lost my leg last spring, but as you can see, I get around pretty well!"

"Do people stare and ask what happened to you?" Annie asked.

"Yes, they do. At first it used to bug me, but now I don't let it get to me. Sometimes I even get extra attention and treats. Besides, once I stopped feeling sad and sorry for myself, I realized all the things I can still do."

"Like what?" Annie asked.

"Well, let's see.

I can still run because we only use three legs at a time anyway. That means **I can still chase squirrels.** I never catch them, but I never did when I had four legs either! **I can walk-hop in the woods,** and **I can swim.** That means I can still bother the geese and stir things up in the river. I can still snooze in the sun on my back porch, and I can still roll over and scratch my back on the driveway. I could even roll in horse poop like your gross brother Max, if I wanted to, that is! I can still hear the birds' songs in the spring, **and I can still feel happy and loved** when I cuddle up with my Mom and Dad in their bed. It's still a sweet dog's life."

"Do you ever miss your leg, or feel that it's still there?"

"Sure, but it doesn't make me feel better to yearn for it. Some things you just have to let go . . . so you can go on," said Sam.

"Thanks, Sam. I'll think about all those things . . .

Whoa, what a great smell! Come over here and take a sniff." The two dogs walked on together down the path, sniffing and exploring.

Meanwhile, Max had been kept on his leash so he wouldn't bother the two older dogs. He strained and pulled hard until Mom had had enough. He heard Mom say to her friend that she was going to get him a personal dog trainer (whatever that was), to discipline him and teach him manners.

Manners, discipline, that didn't sound good.

Just then the moms called Annie and Sam back to the cars. Before Annie left Sam, she said, "I have one more question, Sam. Hope you don't mind. Do you think my scrawny, dirty, smelly, stinky, loud mouth, brother Max, is cute?"

Sam laughed. **"You've got to be kidding!"** she said as she hopped into her car.

As they drove home Annie chuckled, "You see Max, you are not as irresistible as you think!"

Max's pride was only slightly and temporarily wounded. After all, he had lots of other girlfriends chasing after him, and he knew he was cute.

More than anything, he was just happy to see Annie laughing again.

Annie may have lost her leg, but she had found her way back to her life.

ideas for writing

Why was it important for Annie to meet Samantha? Could Sam understand Annie's fears better because she had lost her leg too?

Who helps you when you are afraid or anxious?

Do you know someone like Max? What does that person or animal do to make you laugh?

How can Annie be happy even though she had cancer and lost her leg?

ideas for writing

Annie and Max have lots of adventures in real life and in my imagination. Use your imagination to create an Annie and Max story. (Hint, Max is usually in some kind of trouble, and Annie uses her "smarts" to help out!)

The Real Max and Annie

Max and Annie are English Springer Spaniels who live in Chagrin Falls, Ohio.

Max is two years old, or 14 in dog years. Max was a terrible terror of a puppy. He chewed pants and pillows; he dug holes and chased moles, and he never came when he was called unless he was real hungry. He was hit by a pick-up truck, lost in the woods in a snow storm, rescued when he fell through the ice in a swamp, pecked on by a gaggle of geese, and almost caught in quick sand. He is lucky to be alive!

Annie thinks he is a pain most of the time, but sometimes he has a good idea, like raiding the trash or picking the roasted chicken off the kitchen counter. She likes it too because he always gets blamed.

Annie is Max's dog big sister. She is 9 years old or 63 in dog years. She has always been well-behaved, well-bred, and well-trained. She was almost the perfect puppy. When she was twelve weeks old she chewed a tiny hole in the arm of the new leather chair, and later that week she spilled a whole bottle of pancake syrup on the kitchen floor. That was eight years ago; she hasn't done anything naughty since!

We know she loves Max because they sometimes "talk" to each other and kiss when she is in the mood. Annie is the boss of Max, but he doesn't care because all he wants to do is hunt, chase, run, swim, eat, and get lovies from the family.

In December, 1998, Annie had her left front leg removed because she had cancer. This book is her story, and a lot of it is based on real events and characters.

Visit both dogs on our web site *maxandannie.com*.

imagination page Use your imagination on this page! You can draw Annie and Max playing with your pet, write a poem, make a puzzle, draw a map to a secret place or just doodle. Have fun.

coloring page

Color Max playing ball. He is brown and white, but you could make him purple if you want!